For Freya, with love – G.A.

For my brother, Donald – K.P.

Endpapers by Charlotte Farrell, aged 7

Korky Paul would like to thank
St Mary's and St Peter's CE Primary School, Teddington,
for their help with the endpapers

PUFFIN BOOKS
Published by the Penguin Group: London, New York,
Australia, Canada, India, Ireland, New Zealand and South Africa
Penguin Books Ltd, Registered Offices:
80 Strand, London WC2R 0RL, England
puffinbooks.com
First published 2012
009

www.korkypaul.com

OOPS

Sir ScallyWag

and the GOLDEN UNDERPANTS

GILES ANDREAE

KORKY PAUL

PUFFIN

Long ago there lived a king
Of majesty and fame,
The mighty king of England . . .
    And King Colin was his name.

King Colin wasn't clever
And King Colin wasn't bold,
But what made King Colin special
Were his underpants of gold.

Now one night, while the king and queen
Were sleeping in their bed,
A giant stole these underpants
And put them on his head.

Next morning, when King Colin
Went to put his tunic on,
He stared down at the floor and cried,
"My underpants! They're gone!

"They're my underpants of glory,
My underpants of power!
My breakfast will be ruined
If they're not back within this hour!

"Go, send out for my bravest knight,"
He bellowed down the hall.
And so they fetched Sir Scallywag,
The bravest knight of all.

Sir Scallywag was mighty
And Sir Scallywag was bold.
It didn't seem to matter
He was only six years old.

"What is it I can do for you,
O mighty king?" he cried.
"Retrieve my golden underpants,"
The trembling king replied.

"I'm lost without my underpants,
My underpants of gold.
And, besides, it's rather draughty
And my bottom's getting cold."

"Your wish is my command, O king,"
Sir Scallywag declared.
"I promise on my life
The royal bottom won't be bared."

He whistled for his trusty steed
Who cantered to his side.
"Come, Doofus," said Sir Scallywag.
"We're going for a ride!"

They galloped over mountains
And they rode through forests green,
But, alas, the golden underpants
Were nowhere to be seen.

"Disaster!" cried Sir Scallywag.
"What will King Colin do?
He'll probably chop my head off
And then flush it down the loo."

So he rode back to the castle
In a state of dread and fear,
But just then, on the horizon,
Something started to appear.

A giant on a jet-black horse
Came riding brave and bold.
And there, upon his helmet,
Shone the underpants of gold!

"I've come to take this kingdom,"
The wicked giant said.
"And no one can defeat me
With these pants upon my head!

"And when I've beaten every knight,
Which won't take too much time,
I'm going to storm the castle
And this land will all be mine!"

"Oh, will it?" cried Sir Scallywag.
"Well, let's just wait and see,
For you won't defeat this kingdom
Without first defeating me!"

The giant roared with laughter,
"But you're just a little boy!
I could kill you in an instant.
I could break you like a toy."

"Just try it," said Sir Scallywag,
While lowering his lance.
"Let's show him what we're made of.
Come on, Doofus, boy! ADVANCE!"

The giant started galloping
And bellowed out with glee,
"I'm going to slice you up, young knight,
And toast you for my tea!"

"Oh, crikey!" gulped Sir Scallywag.
"Quick! Think! I need a plan . . .
How ever can I overcome
This stinkpot of a man?

"My lance won't even reach him
On that giant jet-black horse . . .
My lance . . ." He stopped, then smiled and said,
"My lance . . .
       my LANCE!
             Of course!"

Then, suddenly, amidst the crowd,
There came a creaking sound.
Sir Scallywag had thrust his lance tip
Deep into the ground!

And all the king and queen could do
Was raise their heads and stare
As Scallywag was catapulted
High into the air!

He soared above the giant.
"Now, take this, you oaf!" he said,
And he smashed his armoured bottom
Hard against the giant's head.

The giant tumbled from his horse,
And off his helmet rolled.
He scrabbled through the dirt
To grab the underpants of gold.

Sir Scallywag had got there first
And shouted through the cheers,
"Just leave them there, you numpty,
Or I'll chop off both your ears!"

Sir Scallywag then raised the pants
To show that he had won.
They glittered and they sparkled
In the brilliant evening sun.

"Oh, no!" the giant sobbed and wailed,
"I'm scared! I want my mum!"
And, crying like a baby,
He began to suck his thumb.

"Oh, thank you, brave Sir Scallywag,"
Rejoiced the king and queen.
"You're the bravest little fellow
That this kingdom's ever seen!

"No other knight we've ever known
Has shown such splendid form."
Then the king sat down for breakfast . . .
And his eggs were still just warm!

So, boys and girls, remember this –
Although you may be small . . .
Have courage, and you too can be . . .

The bravest knight of all!